# Sand Dollar Island

Also by Rob Smith:

Novels:
*Children of Light*
*McGowan's Call*
*McGowan's Retreat*
*McGowan's Return*
*McGowan's Pass*
*Shrader Marks: Keelhouse*

Criticism:
*Hogwarts, Narnia, and Middle Earth*

Poetry:
*256 Zones of Gray*
*Mzungu, Hello*
*The Immigrant's House*

# Sand Dollar Island

## Rob Smith

**Drinian Press/**
Huron, Ohio

This book is a work of fiction. As such, names, characters, incidents, and places (real or imagined) are used fictitiously and are products of the author's imagination. Any resemblance to persons or actual events is coincidental.

*Copyright © 2013 by Robert Bruce Smith*
All rights reserved. No part of this book may be scanned, reproduced, or distributed in printed or electronic form without permission.

Illustrations by the author

Drinian Press, LLC
P.O. Box 63
Huron, Ohio 44839
Visit our Web site at: www.DrinianPress.com

Library of Congress Control Number: 2013930201

Smith, Rob- 1947

ISBN-10: 0983306974
ISBN-13: 978-0-9833069-7-9

Printed in the United States of America

# Sand Dollar Island

*To Richard Bach*

# Chapter 1

# Change of Venue

The collision was unavoidable. Jeff saw it rolling toward him in a slow-motion unfolding of time that many have described, but remains a cliché to those who have not experienced it firsthand.

He had just attained the crest of the blacktopped washboard of a road, and was greeted by the headlamps and grill of a red Chevy accelerating on the wrong side of a double yellow line. In the eternity of that moment, he saw everything–the look of horror in an opposing driver, the swerve of the car being passed as its operator trounced on the brakes of a silver-gray Honda, and the red and blue stripes of the Ohio Plate that announced the arrival of a automobile transformed into a two-ton battering ram.

There was no fear in that time, but Jeff wondered what it would be like to die alone. He turned aside to look at the empty passenger's seat to his right. Ten minutes earlier, his wife would have been there beside him, but the seat was no longer there. In retrospect, he would say that the seat might have still been there, but it was obscured by a shimmering wall. That description was not fully accurate, but this was one of those edges of reality at which words no longer function properly.

The shimmering might have been a wall or a curtain or a veil or none of those things at all. Some might have called it a trick of light, that is, if light is given to sleight-of-hand illusions. All Jeff knew was that it was some sort of safe cover. If he could cross over the center console of his small car, he could climb into a safe place beyond the shimmering light or wall or tunnel. Of course, he could not move quickly, strapped in as he was with a shoulder harness and seat belt. He would have to be granted a contortionist's skill in any case to manage the tumble over the gearshift and into the vacant upholstered well. He suspected that the actual deathblow would be preceded by an airbag deploying like an exploratory left jab in preparation for the knockout that would follow when the four cylinder engine of his car would attempt to occupy the same time and space as a V-6 from General Motors.

But all of a sudden he was moving. Unaware of any unbuckling or straining, he jumped from his place beside the wheel, but not toward the seat but to the cover of the shimmering. It was not a matter of crawling or contorting, it was more like running full tilt toward a place where the fog was just lifting along the edge of a shore. And so he ran to the safe place.

At first there was only silence in that place. He wondered if he was, in fact, dead, but he was breathing. He was sure enough of that; he was seeing clearly as well. The cornfields that had bordered the country road had been displaced with a shoreline that now sounded with the regular pulse of water surging and retreating against a smoothly pebbled coast.

How far had he been thrown? He looked behind him back toward the car, which was no longer there. There was, however, that same strange light sparkling like a patch of cellophane suspended from nothing over a patch of bank gravel.

Jeff walked toward it. It appeared to be nothing in the sense that it was less substantial than the water and the stones and the sky, all of which seemed distinct and well defined. He walked in a ring around the light thinking that at some point in his circle, his body would block the projecting source like a shadow passing in front of a prism, but the source of the phenomenon must have been contained in itself because it seemed unaffected by anything in his surroundings.

Where was he? Where was the road, the car, or the double yellow line? The nearest water was on the shores of Lake Erie, but this did not feel or smell like a freshwater lake. A sand dollar, or something very like one, had washed up along the shore. He reached down to pick it up. It was coarse in his hand like a disk of pumice, just as the echinoderms were along the Carolina coast that he remembered from springtime vacations to Kiawah Island.

Where *was* he?

He suspected that the answer was in the shimmering. He walked back to the spot where the light still hovered above the water-smoothed stones of the beach. Something told him not to pass a hand through it. It might have been some sort of silvery fire, but it did not burn when he ran through it on the way to this strange new *here*.

"Jeff."

He heard his name and tried to find the speaker, but he was quite alone.

"Jeff, can you hear me?"

It sounded like his wife's voice. "Sam?" he said.

"I think he tried to say my name," said Samantha.

"It could just be a reflex," said a more authoritative voice. "There's been a lot of brain damage. I doubt if he can hear you."

Jeff knew that the voices came from the shimmering.

"I'm sure he can hear me," Sam insisted. "Even with that tube in his mouth, he's trying to say my name."

"Don't get him excited," said the other voice, but she did not seem to listen or care.

"Jeff, Honey, you can't talk now. You're on a respirator. If you can hear me, squeeze my hand."

Jeff felt something and looked at his empty left hand. Nothing was there, but he had felt the pressure of familiar fingers, Sam's fingers. As if an unspoken permission had been granted, he reached through the shimmering and his hand disappeared from his wrist in the sunlight of that place.

Someone on the other side took it, and though the meeting was tender, it drew him back out of sunlight and into pain. No, it wasn't pain exactly. It was fog, a disorienting distortion of thought that nauseated and contorted his feelings.

"He squeezed my hand," said a voice playing at the wrong speed. "That's a good sign, isn't it?"

"It's too soon to tell."

## Chapter 2

## Samantha's Return

The swirling universe only added to the impulse to barf, but movement was restricted by straps and by a hose taped to his cheeks and forehead. The restrictions could not, however, convince a stomach to settle in time to avoid the acrid taste that flooded his mouth.

"Suction!" A plastic probe inserted itself from somewhere and hissed until it caught the flood of vomit.

Jeff tried to catch an image from the whirligig that replaced sky and sea and beach. The shimmering curtain might have been in the flashing images, but Samantha's tearful face was for certain. He anchored on that image like a figure skater picking a focal point while spinning on the ice. It brought him back and the room stopped.

He tried to catch his breath, but it was not his to catch as the intubation forced his chest to heave against his will.

"He's trying to breathe on his own," said a disembodied voice. It was not Samantha's. Her lips did not move, except to kiss a hand that she raised to meet them. It was his hand. He could feel it now.

The owner of the disconnected voice must have done something to the machine because it started to pick up his pattern of breaths. It insisted, however, on taking in more air than broken ribs wanted, and offered no choice. He'd begin a breath and the machine would inflate him.

"We're going to tranquilize him now so that he won't fight the machine."

*No, just take me off the damn machine*, thought Jeff as his senses returned, but thoughts are softer than whispers and already he sensed a new turning force like a strong arm had just reached out to spin the merry-go-round that he was riding. He looked quickly for a focal point as Sam's face blurred past. Then he saw the shimmering. He dove for it leaving the tubes and machines like he had his seatbelt harness. He passed through in one bound and found himself in the sunshine of a better day.

## Chapter 3

## The Iguana Speaks

At first, he thought the place unaltered, but then he realized that several things had indeed changed. First, there was a gold disk lying on the edge of the surf where a ribbon of sand formed a barrier between the water and the smooth round stones of the cobbled shoreline. Second, there was a lizard of some sort seated on a boulder maybe fifteen yards off the beach. It was facing away from the water and toward a point where heavier vegetation had established a foothold against the tidal surge. It was the first living animal he had seen in that place.

*The sand dollar must have been alive once*, he thought. But where was it now? He remembered picking it up and was pretty sure that it was at the exact spot where there was now a golden disk. *It must be a trick of the light*, he thought moving toward it. *I must have dropped it and the sun-bleached shell reflects gold from here.* But he was wrong.

As he moved closer there was no transformation to white. When he reached down to touch it, his hand passed through the color and found only the sand beneath it. It was some sort of hologram, color and shape without substance.

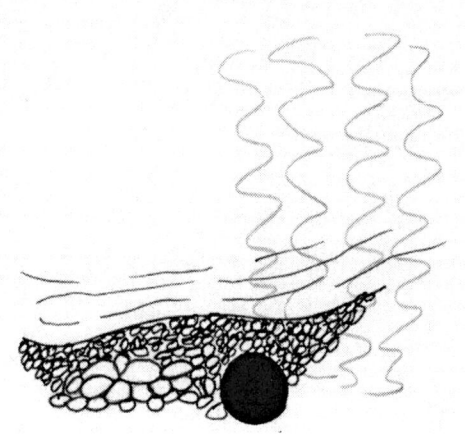

"It's a spot marker," observed a guttural voice that sounded as if it had not spoken for a very long time.

Jeff turned to face the sound, but saw no speaker.

"You were here before, weren't you?" said the voice. It seemed to be coming from the lizard that had turned toward him and away from underbrush. "You were here before," it repeated, "and you took something from that spot."

"I suppose I did," answered Jeff. "I didn't realize that I was doing anything wrong."

"I can't say whether it was wrong," said the lizard, "it's just what you did. Tell me, are you a Grieve?"

"I don't know what that is."

"I don't exactly know either," said the reptile. "They come here just like you did, then refuse transportation, and go back further from the sea."

"Have there been others?"

"Did you think you were the first?"

Jeff thought for a moment. "I have not thought about this at all. It's something that just seemed to happen. I keep jumping back and forth between two places. This one seems the safest, at least for now. Sam is waiting for me there, but there's a wall of machines that keep us from talking."

The lizard did not seem thrown by the mention of Samantha's name or maybe it was just indifferent to descriptions that came from somewhere outside its reality. It tilted its head toward Jeff as if trying to adjust into binocular vision. "No boat came for you."

Now it was Jeff's turn to be confused.

"Should there have been one?"

"Usually is. Comes right up to the shore. Humans climb on like they've been expected or see somebody they know already on board. The Grieves just back off. When the ferry leaves, they usually head inland fearing that another boat will come along and snatch them off the beach."

"Does that happen?" asked Jeff turning warily toward the open sea.

"I've never seen or heard of it, but they're afraid nonetheless. It might be something they'd do if they had the chance. I know they try to snatch us."

"*Us?*"

"Those who live here!" said the lizard as if Jeff had just asked the dumbest thing ever.

"I'm sorry," he said, "it's just that I've not seen much in the way of life here. I found a sand dollar, but that was just a shell. And now, you."

"And you've taken the shell out of this world, and its place is marked so that you'll remember to bring it back; do you have it with you?"

Jeff was pretty sure that he didn't, but everything had happened in such dramatic fashion that it might still be in his hand. It wasn't. That was the hand that Sam had kissed in a surgical suite in another place. "No," he said, "I must have dropped it."

"It seems like I have lived here forever," began the reptile, "and have never seen this before." Again, Jeff was confused.

"Never seen what?"

"A human without a ferry. A human who took something away. A human who came back and still there is no transportation arranged. I don't think you're a Grieve. They turn away from their rescue. You weren't offered any. I told the others that you weren't a Grieve, and that's why I came out to speak with you."

"So, you don't talk to Grieves."

"Too dangerous, even for an iguana and we're too ugly to eat."

Jeff laughed at the way this was stated. The iguana did not take any offense and joined with a less than melodious chortle. "So the Grieves turn down a boat ride and then start looking for food."

"That's pretty much it. Don't seem to know any better. They don't understand this place and so they try to live by the rules of the place they came from."

"What is this place?"

"For us, it's become a home. That's plain and simple. For folk like you, well, I'm not exactly sure. Seems like it's where humans get sorted out."

"Sorted out?"

"They're either Grieves or Travelers. The Travelers get on the boats that come for them; the Grieves stay and wait."

"What are they waiting for?"

"Can't really say for certain. Some wait to go back. Some wait to be led somewhere else. Some have old arguments that they want to live in different ways. We just stay clear of them, at least when they first arrive. After they've been here awhile they get less dangerous to us and more dangerous to each other."

"How do they get less dangerous to you?"

"They stop trying to eat us. That's why we stay clear of the newest Grieves. They start trying to kill us about the time that they start worrying about their next meal. By most accounts, iguanas are too ugly for snacking."

"Unless they're really hungry," offered Jeff in a teasing tone.

"They're never really hungry, though."

"Wait long enough…"

"Are you hungry? Are you hungrier now than when you arrived two weeks ago?"

"Two weeks? It's been less than an hour!"

"You'd better ask Samantha," said the iguana. "She'd know better. The Grieves stay on this island until they die or until a boat comes for them."

"They die? What kills them? Do they starve without knowing it?"

"They do not starve," said the reptile. "None of their old needs matter here. They die on the inside from old dreams and ancient hurts. You, on the other hand have this…" He shuffled his short legs clockwise until he was squarely facing the shimmering.

"What is it?" asked Jeff.

"Your way out," said the animal. "Ask Samantha."

## Chapter 4

# Uno

"The occupational therapist says that you're doing much better when you play Uno!" It was Samantha who had just entered the room. Her voice was cheery, but Jeff knew her well enough to know it was an act. "She's going to add more numbered cards in the deck tomorrow. You'll be playing with zeros, ones, twos, and threes tomorrow. Not just zeros and ones."

He vaguely remembered putting down cards face up trying to match colors or numbers with the card of his opponent. More clearly, he remembered the unlikely conversation with a reptile on a beach where he could move and talk freely.

He could not move so well here. He didn't feel that his wrists were attached to anything, but his right leg was stiff and suspended from a chain attached to a rail at the end of the bed. His left arm was stiff as well.

"How many baskets were under the bridge?" he asked. As he heard the words, he knew they were wrong. He had meant to ask, *How many days has it been?* Words in his brain, however, didn't seem to know the way to his mouth. Samantha sensed his frustration.

"The doctor says that the head injury has affected your speech. The therapy will help, just be patient."

*Be patient?* he thought. He had to tell her about the shimmering which, even now, was on the right side of the bed, near the window that looked out over a flat white-gravel roof landscaped with ductwork and air handlers.

"See the umbrella," he said gesturing to the silvery curtain. Samantha looked out the window.

"No need for an umbrella today. Only sunshine." She leaned over to give him a quick kiss, then settled in a chair she'd drawn close to the bedside. Opening her canvas tote bag, she pulled out a short pencil and a flimsy book of Sudoko puzzles.

Jeff waved his right hand frantically in the direction of the pencil. "The butterscotch," he said.

She looked at the yellow pencil. *Butterscotch* might have been the right color. "Do you want the pencil?"

He nodded. As she handed it to her, she also retrieved her bag which contained a small yellow note pad. She held it directly under his now penciled right hand.

*How long have I been here?* he wrote in a shaky hand which had as much to do with her unsteady support of the pad against the point of the lead as with his writing skill.

"Nurse!" Samantha took the pad with her as she ran from the room. Her exclamation drew the duty nurse from the station. "Look," she said waving the pad at the nurse as he entered the room."

"That's fantastic!" said the attendant. "His brain is working, he's just getting his words confused. Did you tell him?"

"Tell him what?" she asked.

"How long he's been here!"

"Oh! I'm sorry, I just got so excited."

Jeff could sense that this emotion was real and not an extension of the *cheery-enter-the-room* tone.

"Let's see..." she began before the nurse stopped her short.

Turning to Jeff, he asked, "Are you following our conversation?"

Jeff nodded and was pleased when they smiled in unison. Apparently, he had bobbed his head in the *yes* direction. He could not be too sure of anything.

"You were four days in intensive care, three days in the step-down unit, and a week here in therapy. Let's see, that's..."

In spite of his apparent low level performance at cards, his mind raced to the mental math answer more swiftly than hers. *That's fourteen days, the iguana was right!*

He started to write that on the pad and then reconsidered. *Butterscotch* had come out of his mouth when he meant *pencil*. If he wrote that a lizard told him it had been two weeks, they would doubt his written words. Instead he wrote: *Can you see the shimmering near the window?*

The confusion on their collective face told him *no*.

"It could be that his vision center has been affected as well," said the nurse to Samantha who nodded her understanding.

"I think this notepad is going to be our good friend for awhile," said Samantha reverting to her cheery voice. "Why don't you write down some of your questions and I'll tell you what has been going on."

*No*, thought Jeff. *I'll write down what has been going on just on the other side of that curtain.* But she couldn't see the curtain, and apparently, it was all in his head anyway.

"Don't get him too excited," warned the nurse. "I'll put a call into the doctor so that she can make a further examination. Take it slow for now."

"Okay," agreed Sam, and the nurse left the two of them alone.

It was a very odd and awkward moment for them both. They had been married for more than eight years. Sometimes they had lain awake all night together talking about the house or the children or about remembering to go outside at two o'clock to watch the Perseid meteor shower. Now he did not know where or how to begin. *The children!* He suddenly remembered Megan and Brent.

*How are the kids doing?* he wrote forgetting that if he went too quickly his scrawl would be as indecipherable as his speech.

"They are afraid," she said, "they're with my mother. They will be so relieved that you can write."

Again, there was that awkward silence. How could he address the events of the past weeks that he himself could not understand? But, quite by accident, she broached the subject.

"When did you start carrying a sand dollar for luck?" she asked. She opened the drawer of the bedside table and withdrew the white disk. Jeff smiled at the proof in his wife's hand.

*I took it from off a beach after the accident,* he wrote. A confused look hijacked her expression.

"After?"

*Don't tell the doctor that my brain injury is causing this. The proof is in your hand. I have been to another place. I took the sand dollar from there.*

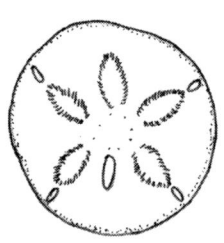

Sam didn't say anything for a long minute. When she did open her mouth to speak, she looked again at the shell in her hand and went silent. At last she framed a careful question. "How did you get there?"

Jeff looked toward the window where he could still see the silvery distortion in the air. Language could not explain what he was seeing to a person who could not share his perspective. *There is a silvery curtain near the window. I know you can't see it, but I can. It was in the car just before the crash and I got through it. I was in that place for two weeks.*

"But you were here all the time. I saw you when they brought you in by ambulance, and when they had you on life support."

*I know,* he offered. *Somehow I leave my body here, but I have one when I'm there. There was no pain in that place.*

"Are you going to die?"

*I don't think so. Not yet.*

# Chapter 5

## Advance Guard

Now that he could communicate, Jeff sent Samantha home to sleep in their own bed instead of moving between the recliner next to his bed and the sofa in the visitors' lounge.

*I'll be fine,* he scribbled quickly. *Go home.* But before the nurse could send him off to morphine-land, he scrambled through the shimmering into the coastal daylight of a distant shore.

Jeff stood looking at the waves under a blue sky. He had been there before, but the light seemed ever the same. He wondered whether the weather, cycles of days, or any of the regular assumptions of seasons held in this place.

"Was the iguana right about your passage of time?" Jeff looked for the speaker whose voice again came from the dense line of vegetation that rimmed the stony strand. The rock where he had seen the lizard was quite empty, and the voice came from deeper back near a sheltering palmetto.

"Over here," said the voice.

This time Jeff recognized a plated mound that could only be the carapace of a giant tortoise. "Oh," he said, "I didn't see you there at first." He marveled that the words he intended to speak came out smoothly and easily.

"Most don't see me at the start," said the animal. "That's why the iguana always goes first when we want to speak with humans."

"I thought it was because he was too ugly to eat," said Jeff.

"Did Handsome tell you that?"

"Handsome?"

"Of course he's handsome. He's the best looking he that ever existed."

The twist of the phrase made Jeff smile. "So you're handsome, too!"

"Of course," said the reptile. "As are you. Don't you agree?"

Jeff laughed again. "I suppose, when you put it that way. Back where I just came from, I'm not much to look at right now."

The turtle didn't answer directly; it just extended a giant, flat clawed foot and paddled counter-clockwise to face Jeff head-on. It seemed to stare into his eyes for a moment so that he turned away to break the attachment. "You don't seem exactly like the other Grieves," it stated at last.

"I have to admit, I don't know what a Grieve is?"

"They like to name things and don't like changing their opinions of the things they've named: *too ugly to eat, too slow to ride, too fast to catch.*"

"Let me guess, you're *too slow to ride.*"

Tortoise beaks don't readily bend into smiles, but their eyes can show delight.

"Yep, that's what they call me. What do you think?"

Jeff considered this, and then said: "you are exactly as fast as you're supposed to be!"

"You are not a Grieve, then. But in all fairness, I have to say that they don't just label us, they label each other, too."

"Like *ugly* and *slow*?"

"Yes. And like *powerful, strong, stupid, weak, guilty,* and *evil.*"

"And probably *fat, skinny, short, puny,* and *nerdy.*"

"Heard them all," said the tortoise. "Can't say that I understand them much. All the Grieves appear to me about the same."

"To you, each one is the best he or she that they are."

"Not exactly," said the reptile. "They *could be* the best, if they just left a few things behind."

"What could they leave behind?"

"The labels! Handsome and I have talked about them many times. Do they have any meaning where you come from?"

Jeff thought about athletes and corporate execs, of lonely kids sitting home on prom nights and shooters who dress like comic book characters then go to malls, schools, and theaters. "Yes," he answered, "sometimes they fit and sometimes they hurt."

"They don't fit here," said the turtle. "They called me *soup* once. Tried everything in their power to get me out of this shell and into a pot." Again, the animal spoke with amusement in its voice.

"Obviously, they didn't succeed."

"Oh, but they tried. After about two days one of them realized that they had no pot and no fire to put it on. Another one just kept complaining that none of the plants or rocks were very good weapons. Finally, one of them asked: *Is anyone hungry anyway?*"

"And they weren't, right? At least, I've never been hungry here," said Jeff. "Handsome was right about my being here for two weeks, but I never saw a sun rise or set."

"And you won't," said the turtle. "This is not a place where anyone is supposed to stay. It's a place to go on from."

"What about you? You live here, don't you?"

"For a time, but time is short and has no bearing on this island. In all, there are three of us Handsomes. You've already met two of us."

"I haven't yet met *too fast to catch*, have I?

"I suspect that you will meet the Grieves before you meet the last of us."

"Why's that?" asked Jeff.

"Because three of them have already seen you!" With that, the tortoise withdrew into itself.

Jeff looked down along the shoreline and saw three strangely shaped figures approaching. He felt easier when he saw the shimmering in its normal place on his right. It would provide a quick retreat if the Grieves proved troublesome. They seemed to be approaching at an aggressive pace, and they were wearing helmets made of straw which provided comic relief from an otherwise serious demeanor.

"Explain yourself," said one who must have been the leader of the trio.

The directive was a bit confusing. How could Jeff explain himself, and why would it be necessary? He was in an odd place which had randomly presented itself to him as it probably had to them. *The best bet*, he thought, *was to avoid the command and start over.*

"Hello," he said trying to mimic Sam's cheery voice. "Can you tell me where I am exactly?"

"You are trespassing in the country of the White Samurai of the Rising Moon," was the answer spoken in unison.

"How's that for a high-sounding label?" said the tortoise in a low tone that echoed from beneath the shelter of his overhanging shell. Jeff was sure that the approaching trio could not hear it over the scrabbling of their feet over the shifting beach stones.

"I didn't realize that I was on anyone's property," he said. "I'm sorry if I offended. I can move on."

"Too late for that," said the man who was obviously the captain of the guard. He was rearranging the shocks of dried marsh grass that was held around his brow by a thin braid of woven stems. Jeff couldn't figure out the exact purpose of the headdress other than to make the three heads look like cylinders or stove pipes of a sort that could not withstand heat, flame, or high wind.

"There are no ships, sir," said a second voice to the captain. This voice sounded female but he/she was also wearing a grass vest as protective armor.

"Good," said the captain. "We'll be safe while we interrogate this one."

*This one?* thought Jeff. *How many strangers do they come across around here?* He had been here for awhile and had seen only two Handsomes. He looked down at the turtle who was more effective at looking like a rock than these three were at looking like a military patrol.

"Why didn't you get on the boat?" said the woman's voice.

"No boat came for me," he answered as if going along with the joke.

"This one is very suspicious," said the captain. "I think we'll have to take him prisoner."

"I haven't done anything," protested Jeff.

"You didn't leave, now did you?" accused the leader.

"I can if you want," he answered.

"Without a boat?" mocked the third. "That, I'd like to see!"

Jeff didn't like the way these Grieves were talking, and was only too glad to oblige. "Okay," he said. "This is how I'd leave." He took three steps and walked through the shimmering back into his hospital room.

## Chapter 6

# Megan and Brent

He found himself sitting up straighter than before, and Jeff realized that he was in a chair rather than chained to the bed. There was a walker to his left and the shimmering to his right.

His impulse to run from the confrontation was suddenly tempered by the sudden awareness that one of the three strangers might have tried to follow him through the silvery portal, but no one else came through to join him. He surveyed his surroundings which were both familiar and alarming. The furniture was the same, but the whiteboard showed that the nurse on duty was Allison rather than the man who was in there when he left. It was also a Wednesday when he had returned to the island, and the note read Tuesday. He had been gone at least six days, maybe longer. The yellow pad and pencil were within reach on the edge of the bed. He took it up and read what he had obviously written while away. The writing seemed weak and flat. *What happened today? Did you talk to the doctor? Did you get caught in the rain?*

As he read through the series of simple questions, the door opened and Samantha's head peered in. "How's your day going?" she said.

"Enough," he said (though he meant to say *good enough*).

"You've been in a bit of a funk since they put the pin in your leg, so I thought you might want some company. The kids are here, if you're up to it."

Jeff smiled the only answer he needed, but punctuated his message with a thumbs-up.

Samantha left for less than a minute, returning with two children following closely behind. "Now be gentle," she warned them. "Your daddy's still pretty sore, but see how good he looks."

The two stepped forward.

"Megan and Brent, you've been growing," Jeff said.

"Mommy," said Megan, "you said that Daddy might talk funny." Samantha could not answer for her tears.

"I said it right," Jeff remarked. It must have been seeing the children that worked its magic because much of his speech suffered a degree of confusion. Nevertheless, the yellow pad remained his friend, and some blank pages were eventually torn free so that Brent and Megan could draw pictures after the excitement of seeing their father was replaced by the reality of a room filled with things that they were not permitted to touch.

"I want to draw something for you, Daddy! What should I draw?" asked Brent.

Jeff tore out two sheets and wrote a single word at the top of each. On one he wrote *turtle* and on the second he wrote *lizard*.

"They can't do that," said Samantha.

"Yes we can," said Megan who chose the lizard and went straight to work.

Jeff also took to the pad in his hand. *When I can put words together again, I'll tell them a story*, he wrote.

"Will it be a happy one?" she asked.

"If I can tell it properly, it'll be very happy."

The children set to work on their drawings, and Jeff was surprised, not by the artistry, but by their awareness of the shapes they were attempting to draw.

"They've been to the children's zoo enough times," Samantha reminded him. He had almost forgotten that in the hazy fog that was his memory. His body seemed so alien to him in this real world, and he was more like himself in the other place, something like an in-between world if the Handsomes were to be believed. He had no reason to disbelieve them.

He wondered what his body did while he was away. He scribbled a question about it to Sam.

"Well," she said after a thoughtful pause, "you have really good days, like today, and like a week ago. Your progress seems slower at times. The speech therapist hasn't given up hope, but he's also not heard anything like when you spoke the kids' names. He says that how well you will do depends on whether some of your neural pathways start firing again. You're using the full deck in Uno now," she added to sound encouraging.

Jeff wondered if his progress would be better if he stayed on the real side of the shimmering. He could only vaguely recall the hospital's therapy schedule and knew that his body-memory was not being served by his adventures elsewhere. Still, strange as it sounded, it was refreshing and easier to be with the tortoise and the lizard with a fast thinking mind *and* free speech, instead of here, where communication was complicated and perplexing.

"I have been going to another place," he wrote on the pad. As Samantha read it, her face fell, and he wished he'd not risked the truth.

"The doctor still thinks that's part of your injury," she said. "The deeper you go into it, the harder it will be to maintain consciousness."

"Sand dollar," Jeff said clearly and distinctly. The words brought a smile back to Sam and head turns from the children.

"Do you want us to draw a sand dollar, too?" asked Megan. They had collected them along the Atlantic coast during a spring vacation.

Jeff nodded.

"I'll do it," said Brent.

"No, I'll do it," said Megan. "It was my idea."

"You can *both* do it," said their mother, "and it was Daddy's idea." She smiled again. "I have one here if you want to trace around it," she added retrieving the echinoderm from her purse.

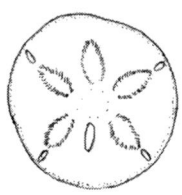

"I've been holding on to it," she said to Jeff. "When you're having a bad…" she tried to take back the word, "when you're having a not-so-good day, I hold it. Sometimes I think it feels warm to the touch. I know that's silly."

*No, it's not*, he scribbled.

After the children had presented their artwork to their father, the time came for them to be returned to the care of grandma. "You were really good visitors today," Sam said to the two who were already well beyond their normal attention span and could descend to meltdown at any moment.

"Excellent company," said Jeff without thinking about the words. Samantha kissed him. He hadn't expected it, and was trying to write one last question.

*What are my bad days like?*

"I should be glad that you're unaware of them, I guess," she began. "Last week when you had that lung infection and didn't bounce back with the breathing treatment, I thought I might lose you. The second antibiotic must have done the trick, though. Thank God for that."

None of that was a part of Jeff's memory. *What was going on? Was he dying? Could he die here while he was talking to the Grieves over there?*

Just then, he was aware that Brent was about to slide off the bed where he had stationed himself for drawing. Jeff's reaction was immediate, but not understood by anyone else in the room. In coming down off the bed, Brent had passed through the shimmering image, and Jeff let out a gasp fearing that his son might be sucked out of the world, but he wasn't. Apparently, this portal was his and no one else's.

"Sorry," he said aloud when the others, in confusion, turned to try and understand his startled reaction. *I thought he was going to fall*, he wrote to cover his real concern.

*The portal was his alone, but would it always be open as a way back?* After his family left, he brooded over this question for a long while. The answer was simple, logical, and strangely discomforting. He would not go through the silvery curtain again. He would stay in the world, work on his therapy, hang onto his family, and get well. The Grieves could not be his concern. They had the three Handsomes who had correctly noted that no boat had come for him when he had reached the island. If the portal closed, what would there be left for him but to weave marsh grass body armor and march around in circles.

His resolve stood every test except the insistence of the shimmering. Getting sleep in a hospital is difficult enough, but that night, it proved impossible. The shimmering intensified. At first it had the annoyance of a blinking neon sign, but the more he ignored it, the brighter it became. When it hit the intensity of the Vegas Strip and showed no signs of abating, he swung his legs over the left side of his bed, gripped his walker, and shuffled out to the nurses' station.

"What are you doing walking without assistance?" A flurry of activity sent staff members to his right and left like spotters beside a trampoline. Jeff looked back down the hallway where the light pouring out of his room seemed to be wheeling into a fireball set to explode in his direction. He couldn't trust his words to sound an alarm, but the expressions on faces told him that *he* was the only spectacle that they were seeing.

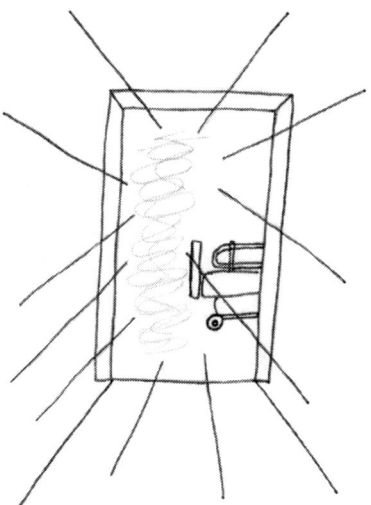

"Are we going to have to tie you down to keep you in bed?"

He shook his head *No*. He knew, however, that it really didn't matter what they did. He had jumped through the restraints on the operating table, and if the shimmering was this insistent, straps would not hold him down.

The hallway was longer than he remembered, and his leg was suddenly aching. He was glad when two others helped him regain his room. They supported him under each arm as they set the walker aside and helped turn him around so that he could sit on the edge of the bed. Once seated, they would help lift his legs and turn him so that he would be lying on his back.

Before they had finished arranging his body, he had left the world. Though they could not feel it, he jumped their grip and was gone.

The sun was shining. It was a clear beautiful day along an open shoreline.

## Chapter 7

## The Grotto

It was apparent to Jeff that he was in the same spot where he always landed. The most distinguishing feature was a golden disk on the edge of the sea which marked the place where he had picked up the sand dollar that now resided in Sam's purse.

It was comforting to know that there was a tangible link between his wife and himself in this remote place. Actually, as he thought about it, he didn't even know if this place was remote. It might only be inches away from the dimensional plane that held his wounded life and precious family. Here, as in the land of his earlier reality, he was limited to senses that saw only within a small spectrum of visible light and within reach of nerve endings and sensory cells.

As beautiful as this day was, there was something unnatural about it, something that he began to suspect from the first. This was not a place at all, at least not a natural place.

Life was not sustainable here. There was no biological web, no food chain seeking a sustaining balance between predator and prey. The iguana had hinted as much. The Grieves began by looking for food until they discovered that they were never hungry. For that matter, Jeff had never been hungry here, or thirsty. *Could the doctor be correct? Could this dimensional reality be a trick of a damaged brain?*

*Even so*, he reasoned, *damaged brains require food and water and I saw that six days passed on a calendar without any.* The plants seemed to be alive, but nothing seemed to be drawn to them and they did not appear to be growing or blossoming. He saw and heard nothing, no buzz of insect, no call of bird, no animal sounds from the undergrowth. While he had found the skeleton of a sand dollar, it was not alive. Since it was one of a kind, it might have been dropped there by another. The turtle and the iguana seemed to be real and alive, but strangely different. In our world tortoises and lizards are mostly silent. A hiss could be possible, but these spoke, as it seemed to his ear, the Midwestern dialect of Noah Webster's English. He wondered if the Handsomes would speak German, French, or Pârsi if he had had a different birth.

Jeff looked up and down the shoreline, out over the water, and back into the line of vegetation. The Grieves would be back under the cover of the plants. If he wanted to avoid them, he should stay near the water's edge. They seemed to fear the boats that might come for them. *Where would the boats take them anyway?* He had come from a place of life where joy touched sorrow, pain and pleasure mixed, and where *dead* meant not alive. Here it was all façade. Everything looked alive, but only a few things were, and they might be alien species on loan from other dimensions.

If the Grieves were right, this was an island, and a walk along the shore would bring him either to an impassible terrain or back to the gold medallion of the sand dollar. He took off his shoes and began to walk through the gentle surf.

After an hour or so, the thought occurred to him that he had no idea how large this island might be. *Australia is an island*, he thought. *Even a small island might be hundreds of miles around.* Still, he did not feel tired, hungry, or parched by the sun which showed no change in position or any inclination to set.

He came at last to a place where the landscape started to rise above the plane of the sea. Boulders were arranged like stepping stones. The stairway might have been crafted by a mason, but more likely, it was a natural feature like the interlocking basalt columns of the *Giant's Causeway* on the northeast coast of Ireland.

In another dimension, he would have considered whether the climb was worth it, but here fatigue grew like the plants: not at all. While the prospect of a better view of the horizon offered some interest, what caught Jeff's eye was a lone seagull halfway up the steps.

*There's the third animal*, he thought. He stepped up onto the nearest and lowest riser. It immediately hopped up a level. *Too fast to catch!*

As he climbed, the bird stayed grounded, maintaining the distance between them. Jeff was beginning to suspect that it was no earthly species of gull, but some flightless variety. That idea disappeared, however, at the highest crest where the bird took to flight in a huge circle out over the water.

"You *are* really too fast to catch," he said aloud.

"Come higher!" called the bird. Jeff assumed that the aviator wanted him to see something across the azure water. Perhaps a boat was coming, *but who would it be coming for?*

When he attained the height, he saw something completely different, a downward staircase like the one he had just climbed. It was part of a rocky ring that enclosed a quiet cove. The water looked clear and deep like a safe anchorage for a deep-draft vessel, but there was more.

Nestled in the stony hillside of the downward slope was a grotto, a rocky cave sheltered under a slab of stone, its front stoop sitting just above the water's edge. The third Handsome lighted on that front landing.

"No need to try and catch me," it said, "I'll wait for you here."

Obviously there was something to see or do inside the grotto, and the only way to prove the premise was to do the deed. Jeff picked his way down the slope, a more arduous task than the climb had been. Still, it was managed easily without sweat or shortness of breath.

"Inside," said the bird when he reached the level where the bird sat hunkered down and showed no interest to hop or flit or fly. "Step inside," it repeated, "there's something that will explain a lot."

Jeff immediately sensed the oddness of the place. Though in the shadow of rock, the temperature inside perfectly matched the outside air. It was as if the thermostat in this universe kept every zone the same. Once his eyes adjusted, the light inside the cave seemed no less dim or bright than the sunshine had been. He easily saw the tightly mitered joints of the smooth gray walls. There were pictographs visible toward the back of the cave which were obviously the *something* that could give him an explanation. He stepped toward the carvings. They were symmetrical but crudely cut. *No,* he thought, *they are finely detailed.*

The truth was that they were both. This may have been the oddest thing yet in this world of oddities. The first impression of the whole was of stick figures, but if you focused on one image within the picture, it morphed into finely cut detail.

The whole was two intersecting lines, one vertical and one horizontal. Where they crossed, was a round white disk. The horizontal line was bookended by stick figures. At the top of the vertical line was drawn a boat of some sort, and at the bottom was a scribbled jumble of lines. There was a carved figure in each of the quadrants defined by the intersection of the lines. In the upper left was a lizard. The upper right held a turtle.

The lower left showed a bird, and in the last quadrant was a person.

Jeff drew a deep breath, not because he couldn't recognize the primitive shapes, but because he had seen some of them before. In fact, the originals had been rendered on paper and resided in his pocket. He reached into his shirt pocket where Megan and Brent had placed their folded drawings. He opened them and made comparisons. They matched right down to the faint lines that Brent had tried to remove with the eraser end of the pencil.

Now he saw that the sand dollar on the kid's drawings matched the disk at the center of the petroglyph. He had not noticed earlier, or it had in fact not been true earlier, that both children's sand dollars were identically rendered. "Why not," he said aloud, "they began with the same traced outline."

"Do you think that would explain it?" asked the gull. "Look at the tortoise on the wall."

The stone rendered version of Brent's two-dimensional half-circle with stick legs, head, and tail began to change. Scales and plates became detailed and the head of the now detailed image turned to make eye-contact. "Did I mention that there are four Handsomes?" it said.

There they were: lizard, turtle, bird, and human. He looked at the last figure fearing what it would show. It too, began to morph into a man looking straight at him and holding papers, two children's drawings. He could actually see the drawings, one was a tortoise the other an iguana and the pictures on the page were changing, growing in detail and precision of line.

"No!" he cried.

"*Yes* is the correct answer," said the bird who had hopped closely beside him.

"That is not me, it can't be."

"How did you get here?" asked the bird. In all honesty, Jeff did not know except for the shimmering. He looked quickly to his right and it was still there. He could jump back. He wanted to, but the bird gave one last instruction. "Look at the scribbles at the bottom."

Jeff looked at the indecipherable jumble of lines which began to swirl before his eyes. There was metal in there and upholstery and plastic. There were three streaks: a thick one of white and thinner ones of red and blue. Then the words swirled into focus: *Ohio, the birthplace of aviation.*

He jumped.

The sweat he had not worked up in that world poured out of him now. His heart was pounding, and he could not catch his breath.

"I thought we lost him that time," said a voice overhead.

## Chapter 8

# Child's Play

"How are you feeling?" Samantha was not in *cheery-voice* mode today. Instead, she was guarded and afraid.

"Better," he said. "I'm feeling better this morning." He heard the right words coming out of his mouth and was amazed, but not as much as Sam was.

"All of a sudden, I believe you!" she said wiping back a stray tear.

"What last night?" he said realizing that he could not push his speech-luck too far without destroying the one sentence gift of hope that he had given her. She didn't seem concerned with his Pidgin English, however, and went on like the sentence structure and the lie about feeling better were true. The fact was that he felt like he was back in the early days of the accident. Physically, he was more tired than pained, but emotionally living in fear that the shimmering would demand his return with sirens and lights. At the moment, at least, it was silvery, silent, and waiting.

"It was a clot," she began. "They said it could have broken free from any one of your injuries. I guess it was small and went to your lung rather than your brain." With this she paused and swallowed hard. "Anyway, they did a procedure. They put it some kind of stent that strains out clots or dissolves them. They put it in through your leg, that's why they have the weight on your thigh. They have to make sure you form a clot at the small incision so that you don't bleed through the nick they put in your artery."

Jeff understood the drill. His father had once had a heart cath. Thin the blood to prevent clots, and pile on the bricks to prevent bleeding. He wanted to come back with a wisecrack, but feared that his words wouldn't pass the clever test. He just nodded.

The pressure on his leg was midway between uncomfortable and annoying, and he was glad when Samantha started to rummage through her canvas tote bag. He smiled at the fact that its regular use had been to contain snacks and games to occupy restless children; now, apparently, he was the one who was supposed to be amused with child's play.

"The kids drew more pictures for you," she said. "They thought they could do better than their first attempts. Of course, Megan thought she could do a better turtle and Brent swore he knew more about lizards."

Jeff began to get an uneasy feeling about the rabbit that Samantha was about to pull out of her hat, even if it was a drawing rather than a bunny, and a bag and not a hat. It was not the sort of magic that he was in the mood for seeing.

"Megan thought that since tortoises and lizards are reptiles, she should add a snake to complete the set." She unfolded a piece of typing paper and handed it to Jeff.

"That's an iguana," he remarked.

"We had to go to the Internet and she thought she'd make it *fancier*–that was her word. Actually, I think she also said more *handsome*, too. Not my idea of handsome, what do you think?"

*He's the best looking he that ever existed*, is what he thought, but given the state of his language skills, it would have sounded strange. "It's good," he said.

"Your speech is so much better today," she said. "Now Brent took a different tack. He decided that although they were all reptiles, they also evolved from dinosaurs. (He didn't like Megan's pile of snakes anyway—said it looked like spaghetti."

*Or a car wreck*, thought Jeff who almost expected to see an Ohio license plate morph out of the tangled lines.

"Anyway, he added a bird! We have a smart kid for a son. Said that birds came from dinosaurs, too." She placed a second sheet into his shaking hand.

Brent had folded the paper in half vertically and then horizontally to create four quadrants. With a straight edge he ran his pencil along the creases to give definition to the areas. On the top left, there was an iguana (obviously modeled from the same Internet jpeg). Next to it was a turtle. Left on the lower level was a gull, and on the right was a man.

Jeff laughed nervously and took the yellow pad from the bedside table. He did not trust his words or his voice. They might betray him. *Why does he have a human in with his dinosaurs?* he wrote.

"Oh," said Samantha, "that's supposed to be you. He said you'd understand."

## Chapter 9

## Silent Watchers

Bed, even a hospital bed, felt good. This was Jeff's first moment to try and put perspective on events from both sets of reality. He had no reason to doubt Samantha's uneasiness about his medical condition. It was confirmed by the anonymous voice above his head when he burst back from the island. *What would have happened if he had died here while he sat studying a pictograph there?* He didn't really want to know the answer, but he suspected that a boat would come to transport him to a place feared by the Grieves. Even so, any place at all had to be better than sharing their mundane existence as captives on the island.

The shimmering was quiet, as if respecting the seriousness of the last episode. Taped to the closet door, however, was a pretty fair facsimile of the image carved in the grotto, and these, from the hands of his own children, seemed to seal his fate in triplicate. Still, Megan and Brent had left out three images from the original fresco, the boat at the apex of the vertical line and stick figures at each end of the horizontal.

Though he had never looked closely at the last pairing, he knew who they were. If he had stared closely at them, he was certain that all the silly details would emerge and they would be men and women sheathed in dead grasses and marching around like an army of clowns. They were the Grieves.

The four central figures were clearly the four Handsomes. He was one, though he had no idea of what that meant. The others seemed to be guardians, but guardians of what? The island? The Grieves? Each other? They were linked, at least in the picture, by the sand dollar. There was only one of those and it was to be returned, its place marked by a golden disk of color but not substance. As far as Jeff knew, the white disk had found a new home tucked away in a corner of Samantha's purse.

The intersecting lines of the compass rose must have held some significance. The *north* position was the boat. The *south* position was the twisted wreck of a car, his car. The connecting line indicated a direct path between his accident and the transportation away from that place that seemed to be not-a-place. The horizontal line, by contrast, seemed to go nowhere. The Grieves were caught there along an axis both anchored and static.

Jeff tried to recall the words of the iguana. What did it say? *They turn away from their rescue.* It was something about turning down their boat passage.

"Do you think he's solved it yet?" asked a voice from the night stand.

"Give him time. He'll figure it out," said another.

"There isn't a lot of time! That's something that he hasn't got."

The last comment chilled Jeff's blood and he turned to see what he had already guessed. The iguana on Megan's paper was talking with the tortoise on Brent's. The drawings were propped up on the nightstand, one against a water pitcher, the other against a plastic cylinder with a blow-tube that the nurse made him use to clear his lungs. Above them both, the gull, which had freed itself from the paper, was flying overhead.

It was the sort of thing that he would have expected to see if he had actually swallowed the oral morphine that the nurse provided. Jeff, however, had grown proficient at palming his pain medications and avoiding the fuzziness of mind that he thought the source of his *island visits*. The pain had not been so bad. More upsetting was the knowledge that drugs could not be blamed. It was either brain damage or reality, not both. As distressing as it might have sounded to a sane person, he hoped that it was head trauma and something that played out only on the little stage between his ears. That was not true, however, and he knew it. A sand dollar in a purse said so, and now, three animated children's drawings did as well.

"What do I need to do?" he asked.

The shimmering to his right began to grow brighter.

## Chapter 10

# The Dungeon

There were no new surprises greeting his arrival on the sunny shores of the calm sea. Nothing changed in this place except the wanderings of the few inhabitants of the island. Jeff suspected that even that roaming followed repeatable patterns, and the approach of three Grieves in their grass shirts confirmed this suspicion.

"Explain yourself," said one who must have been the leader of the threesome. This was exactly the same greeting as had been offered by the earlier patrol, and he considered that it must have been the standard military protocol for the clown army.

As before, the directive was still unclear. After all, what was there to explain? But this time there was a different confusion. He now knew that he was one of the Handsomes, and had some role to play in this farce. What role that was he could not exactly explain, but if he had understood the pictograph even a little, it involved the Grieves. Because of this, he resolved to avoid the quick escape and follow the patrol into the interior of the island.

"Hello," he said, "my name is Jeff and I just arrived here a few minutes ago." He watched the three for some reaction to his comment. If they were the same three as before, they might suspect that, while it was technically true that he had *just* arrived, he had been there before, three times, to be exact.

"You are trespassing in the country of the White Samurai of the Rising Moon," was the answer spoken in unison. (He had also heard this chorus before in the earlier performance.)

"You know what you have to do," said the tortoise in a soft whisper. It quietly sat on the ground nearby and was doing its best imitation of a rock. The Grieves, in their pantomime of high alert, did not hear or see.

"I didn't realize that I was on anyone's property," he said. "I'm sorry if I offended. I would be glad to offer my apologies to the Samurai."

"The White Samurai of the Rising Moon," the man corrected. "Of course you'll come," he said with a nervous attempt at a cruel laugh. "We are armed and you are not! How could you escape?"

Truth was that he had escaped this situation very easily by leaping through the shimmering that he could still plainly see to his right. The three were dressed in much the same way as the earlier patrol, though he suspected that these were not the same three. As they stood there, they nervously rearranged the shocks of dried marsh grass that served as helmets and body armor.

*I don't think they fully trust their military hardware*, thought Jeff, as he tried to ascertain what part of their attire constituted an actual weapon. They each held a single long dried reed which might have once been a cattail in our world. He tested his theory by stepping back and out of their reach. As if by command they all raised the sticks as if they were hafted spears

"You say that you just arrived, but I see no sign of any ship. Did you send it away?"

"No," he answered, and the soldier turned to his fellows as if to see if they heard a lie in Jeff's answer.

"There are no ships, sir," said a second voice to the captain. As before, this voice sounded female but not the one he had heard earlier.

"Stand tall," said the captain. Jeff didn't know whether he was speaking to him or to the patrol. He straightened his shoulders in case the command was meant for him. The two others did as well.

"It's unusual that no boat came for you," said the captain. "Very unusual."

"Sir, if I may," said the third. "Remember about ten years ago when Careless, Stupid, and Blind-fool came back from patrol saying that they had approached a stranger like this and then he vanished?"

"Yes, I remember well," said the leader. (Jeff wasn't sure that he remembered anything.) "And they have been in the dungeons ever since. "Were you here ten years ago, and did you vanish when our patrol came to arrest you?"

*Are these multiple answer questions? No, I was not here ten years ago; yes, I did vanish*, thought Jeff. Rather than speak his mind, he chose his words: "I was not here ten years ago."

"Good, no funny business then! Remember, we are carrying these." He lifted the reed in his hand that seemed less menacing than a rolled up newspaper. "Lead on!"

"Shouldn't one of you lead?" asked Jeff. "I have no idea where you want me to go." *They haven't done this very often*, he mused.

"Slacker, take the point," the leader said to his second. She walked a wide berth around Jeff as she circled to the head of a line. "I'll go last to cut off any retreat." The shimmering was, however, less that two feet away from him, but retreat was not in Jeff's plan.

"We have been conditioned by rigorous military discipline," said the leader, "do your best to keep up. You may wish that you had taken the lead as I first offered."

Jeff supposed that this last comment was meant to cover the earlier command error, but it was still ridiculous. Equally outlandish was the idea that any of them would be winded. Physical discomfort was alien to this place. In fact, it was a troubling fact that hit him every time he passed back through the shimmering and found his very life in danger. Even now as he walked, he had no sensation or imagination about what might be happening in his hospital room or during his therapy treatments.

He wondered what Samantha and the children must have been going through as he walked with an unnatural spring in his step. Back *there*, he was still assigned an escort even when confined to a walker with yellow tennis balls as cushions on the forward rails.

His current military-hardened escorts were not bearing up so well. Several times they called for a halt to their quick-march, which was really a stroll. Jeff wondered if the exhaustion wasn't just a show being performed for the captain who had referred to one of the guards as *Slacker*.

"I can out march you all!" he bragged.

"You're just in better shape than we are, captain!" Jeff wasn't sure but Slacker may have winked at him to go along with the joke.

"Durned if I ain't!" said the leader proudly. The tameness of the expletive made Jeff wonder how long these Grieves had been maintaining their worthless patrols. He had not heard anyone *durn-and-ain't* in years.

It was during this *rest break* that something else became apparent. They had been walking across a field of grass, or what looked like grass for quite some time. Surely this was a path known to these people, but it was not worn. The vegetation seemed soft enough under foot, but showed no sign of ever having been beaten down or trampled. Out of curiosity, he grasped a blade and pulled. The strong tension against his grip was extraordinary. It did not break the plant or yield up a clod.

"Look," cried the third. He held up a dried blade of field grass.

"How'd you find that?" said the captain. "We've been over this field a thousand times. It probably fell out of my belt. Give it to me!"

"No, it didn't," said Slacker. "I was at the head of the line; you didn't even pass by here yet!"

"I did one other time!"

"Everyone, count," demanded the otherwise submissive Slacker, and it was as if he had invoked the protection of Caesar. The demand for a count sent all three to carefully chosen spaces in the field where they shed their head dressings and weed-vests in order to inventory their crop of grasses.

Jeff was no longer sure he knew anything about what was going on. All their former bravado about his capture and insisting on an audience with some *Moon Samurai* just vanished. For that matter, he could have vanished if he wanted. The shimmering was right there. *How long would it take them to notice him missing?*

"Enjoying the show?" Iguana stepped out from a patch of high grass.

"Hi, Handsome," said Jeff. He nodded toward the trio. "It's obviously a status thing."

"They can't cut it or pull it, so they collect it as if it's the wealth of the universe. The one who has the most…"

"Has what?" asked Jeff to the unpredicated sentence.

"Has the most!" answered the lizard. "It's a joke that Handsome and I tell every now and then. We figure it's a human thing. The one with the most useless stuff only has a lot of useless stuff. Apparently, it makes them winners."

Jeff brushed his hand over the grasses. "Is anything here alive?"

"The Handsomes… and the Grieves, though you wouldn't always know it. They keep measuring themselves by the dead stuff."

The captain took the longest to count his strands, and apparently none were missing. The same was true for the others and the *find* was declared an honest new find.

"They hold to their counts as a high moral obligation," said the iguana.

"Who said that?" said the captain as he was arranging his recovered headband. "Look out! To your weapons, troops!" The three jumped back; their reeds in hand pointing toward the lizard. "Don't move!"

he seemed to be saying to Jeff. "We'll draw off the ugly thing!"

"Too ugly to eat, eh Handsome?" he said winking to his scaly friend.

"Watch this," said the lizard as it reared back on its hind legs, extended its red tongue and flopped the crown of skin on its dorsal side. The three guards tore off across the field. "Don't you think you'd better follow?" it asked nodding toward the moving shapes.

"You want to meet the White Samurai of the Rising Moon, don't you?"

"Thanks," said Jeff. "Now I really have to run!"

"Don't think it will be a problem," said the reptile.

"I don't either." Jeff rose to his feet and began to pace toward the fleeting trio who had begun to slow when they saw they were not being followed. "Tell me, is this Samurai as silly as they are?"

"Nope. He's an even bigger fool!"

In no time, Jeff caught up with his three *captors*, and soon afterward, caught his first glimpse of the *bigger fool*. He was seated cross-legged on the ground with his back toward the approaching foursome.

"He's probably in his house over there," said the captain who pointed toward the seated figure. "He won't be able to see us until we get around to the side with the door."

The comments were perfectly strange to Jeff's ears because they did not match the evidence of his eyes. As he approached, he saw what had to be the bizarre explanation. In an open level area, the Grieves had taken thousands of the small rounded stones from the beach and arranged them in rows and intersecting lines which framed relatively small cubicles.

Jeff was led very carefully outside the line of stones around one corner and then another before stopping in front of a break in the line of stones. This, he presumed was the door. The seated figure looked up and showed surprise, as if he was seeing them for the first time. The captain stepped forward.

"We have brought in a prisoner, sir," he said with a slight bow.

"What is his name? Have you interrogated him?"

"His name is Jeff, but we have not interrogated him fully. We thought you would better know what to ask."

"Very good, captain. You say his name is Jeff. Is that short for Jeffrey?" He turned his gaze to the prisoner.

"Yes, it is short for Jeffrey, but I've always been called Jeff."

"Enough of your insolence! Do we have a list of our *Jeffrey* enemies?"

"We do, Sir," said someone who was looking at his feet to avoid eye contact.

"Where is it, then?"

## Sand Dollar Island

"*Careless* keeps the list, sir," said the captain. "He is in the dungeon serving ten years for letting a prisoner escape."

"Bring him here." The captain gave his salute bow, turned, and started walking between the pebbles that outlined the imaginary building. His circuitous route took him finally to a group of three people huddled together not thirty feet away in a direct path from where Jeff stood.

"What is your last name?" said the *White Samurai of the Rising Moon* to Jeff who noticed that the man was neither clothed in white nor appeared to be a Samurai. Instead, he looked more like a haystack.

*What is your last name?* The question proved a poser. It was something that Jeff could not remember ever knowing. Was this part of his memory that was erased by the accident? He remembered that he had a last name once, but at this moment, having one seemed less important. *What else couldn't he remember?* There suddenly came a daunting list of memory gaps. Along with forgetting his last name was: where he came from, his favorite possession, and whether it was he or Samantha who had won the argument over the nightly set-back on the thermostat. He did, however, remember sitting with Sam, Megan, and Brent on the last evening of their vacation as the sun set over the water, and the plaster-of-Paris handprints that the kids hung proudly on the refrigerator for years.

"What is your last name?" demanded the seated man.

"*Butterscotch*, sir," he said trying to hold a straight face. The shimmering was still radiating peacefully on his right. He supposed that even a vaudeville act could turn ugly, but he still had his way out.

The captain returned. He was followed by a diminutive penitent who Jeff assumed was called or named *Careless*.

"Ah, Careless," began the still seated leader, "this is your opportunity to prove your loyalty. I have captured this *Jeff Butterscotch* and wish to know if he is on the *Jeffreys* enemy list."

The contrite figure turned to Jeff and they recognized each other. It was one of the first patrol members, the one with the woman's voice. She raised her head and struck a thoughtful pose.

"*Butterscotch*," she said, "alphabetically, that would fall between *Bothersome* and *Buzzardfart*. No," she confirmed, "*Butterscotch* is not on the enemies list."

"Excellent," said the Samurai. "How much time remains on your sentence, Careless?"

"Eight years, sir," she said hopefully.

"Well, for your good work today, I reduce your remaining time to five years."

"Thank you, sir," she said bowing while taking two steps back. An escort took her arm to walk her back along the perimeter path to the dungeon.

"As for you, *Strangeface*, I have difficulty believing you are as innocent as you seem. I sentence you to three years."

"Oh Excellency," Jeff said mockingly. "Oh Excellency, if I, your humble servant, may be so bold as to ask, why am I so thusly, imprisoned?"

It was difficult to tell with all the straw falling into the man's face, but Jeff thought he detected a smile.

"Your courtesy serves you well, *Newface*. A year in the dungeon is all you need serve." He ordered the captain to escort the prisoner, but Jeff was too alert to what was happening.

"I think I can find my own way," he shouted back as he took a direct path to where the three had been seated. By walking directly, he would be in the dungeon before *Careless*, under escort, would be back in the huddle. The other prisoners gawked as he stepped over the stone boundary of the imaginary walls.

"You cannot do that!" The White Samurai of the Rising Moon was on his feet shouting. "You must go around! I extend your sentence to twenty years!"

Jeff was impressed that the man was capable of standing. To this point, he had not been sure. He stepped over the first row of smooth stones, stopped, and turned back to see the red-faced haystack.

"You can't see me now," he said, "I am behind the wall!"

## Chapter 11

## The First Mutiny

"How did you have the nerve to stand up to him?" asked Careless when she returned to her huddled comrades.

"Did you see and hear what happened?" asked Jeff. They quickly looked away realizing that they had inadvertently exposed a shameful secret.

"So, you know that there are no walls here," said Jeff.

"We know," said Careless, "but it's dangerous to know such things."

"Why dangerous?" he asked.

"Because there is no way off this island," said one of the other prisoners, "it's just better to go along with…"

"With the insanity?" Jeff completed the thought for the man who seemed afraid to speak the words aloud.

"How do you come and go?" asked Careless. "You were the one we captured ten years ago. You told us your name was Jeff back then."

"It wasn't ten years ago," he corrected.

"How could we tell?" said the man who had been the captain on the original patrol and who was now the least *strawed* among them. "There's no time here, every day is like every other. No, that's not true. There is only one day here."

Jeff fell silent after these comments. Until this point, he had only seen the Grieves as objects of ridicule; now he saw that they were not so different from himself. He looked to his right and felt the comfort of the shimmering that they could not see or pass through. Even if they could pass through a portal that appeared to be exclusively his, what would be there for them? They were dead to that world, and he was not.

An urge came over him to escape at that very moment. He wanted to see his wife and children, he wanted to feel life.

"How did you escape?" This time, Careless was more desperate in asking.

"I'm not exactly sure how it works for me," he said trying to calm his flight response. "The bird, iguana, and tortoise have told me that the boats came for you. They were your way from here. This is not really a place to live."

"But it came and left without us," said the most reticent of the three.

"You did not get on," said Jeff. "Why?"

The captain spoke, "We were afraid."

"Afraid of what?"

"Afraid that we'd lose everything that was ours."

"So you lost everything." Jeff's comment went unanswered for a long time in that timeless place. "What are your names?"

"Careless."

"Stupid."

"Blind-fool."

"Those can't be your names any more than mine is *Butterscotch*." The three recoiled at the statement.

"You lied?" said Careless.

"I frankly don't remember," said Jeff. "He put me on the spot when he asked and realized that it doesn't matter who I was as much as who and what I loved."

The three seemed totally confused by the direction of the conversation, so he redirected it to the boat. "Look," he said, "the three other Handsomes think that I'm here to help you people back to the boat."

"Three whats?" asked Careless.

"The iguana, the turtle, and the bird."

"Too ugly to eat…"

"Too slow to ride…"

"Too fast to catch…"

The litany rolled from their mouths like a rehearsed chorus. "They are an important part of your story," said Jeff trying to restore some gravity to the situation. He reached into his pocket to retrieve the first drawings that Megan and Brent had made. "Look," he said as he tried to arrange them after the fashion of the pictograph.

"What are those?" asked Careless.

"What? You mean these drawings? My children made them and…"

"I had children," she said. "You set those on the ground and I remembered smiling when I went though their school papers once."

"Sometimes their mother and I would get to laughing when they got in trouble. That's when they were very little," said the captain. "They just didn't know better."

"So you had family too?" asked Jeff who was trying to shift into the new direction of the conversation.

"I was a teacher," said the quiet one. "I remember students who would get so excited when they met a new idea."

"Margaret."

"What?" asked Jeff.

"I remembered that my name is Margaret."

"I'm Karl with a K."

"I'm Jorge."

"Pleased to meet you all," said Jeff and there were handshakes all around like it was the very first meeting of family friends after many years of separation.

"Our first job is to go to the cove," said Jeff, "I'm sure a boat will come."

"Don't we have to plan our escape?" said Karl.

"Shouldn't we wait until dark?" offered Margaret.

"Have you ever known it to get dark here? Why don't we just stand up and walk away. What will they do? Spear us with marsh grass!" said Jeff.

"That's only if they can see through the walls," said Karl.

In that instant real human laughter was heard on the island for the first time, at least by the listening Handsomes. They already knew, however, (because the gull had seen it) that there was a boat on the horizon.

"Let's just leave all our grass here on the ground. It's of no use to us, but it will keep them counting and dividing for hours," said Jorge.

"I think it will," agreed Jeff. And the first mutiny was under way.

# Chapter 12

## Second Mutiny

When Jeff and his three escapees arrived safely at the beach, there was as yet no sign of pursuit. Jorge had been correct about the four delaying as they meticulously counted and divvied up the marsh grasses left behind.

"Why is that so important?" asked Jeff. "Did you really think it would protect you in an attack?"

"No," said the captain. "For some reason it was a symbol of rank. The White Samurai insisted on it. That and a horse."

"A horse?"

"Yes, we went on patrol to gather up strangers, but what he really wanted was a horse. He said that he needed one so that he could sally forth in an attack."

"Or get away fast," said Margaret.

"He would talk about it at great length," continued the captain. "He wanted something to ride. I suggested that the turtle was large enough for a man to ride (here he gestured toward the tortoise who was slowly approaching them from the shoreline).

"Let me guess," said Jeff, "but he was *too slow to ride.*"

The three laughed their agreement.

"The boat is in the grotto," called the turtle between strides in its measured pace.

"It talks!" said the captain. Jeff wondered that he did not know this, but then maybe the Grieves were not ready to hear voices from what they thought lower life forms.

"Yes," said Jeff. "He and the lizard and the bird are three of the four Handsomes who have protected you."

"And you have been led from your dungeon by the fourth," said the tortoise who had just come up to within the cluster. "If you walk further along the beach, you'll find iguana guarding what looks like a clutch of eggs. They are the tokens of your passage. Take one, and you may board the boat. There are six of them, one for each of you."

"Six?" cried Jeff. "I only was able to bring out three."

"The passenger manifest is never wrong. There will be six to transport. Here come the other three now."

Jeff looked up and saw the other Grieve patrol approaching. They did not look in the mood to talk, but their fierce appearance was marred by the manner of the attack that they were attempting to mount. They rushed forward in as a phalanx of Greek hoplites, foot soldiers recklessly hurling their bodies into the fighting fray. The problem was that their lowered lances were made of grass and doomed to leave no mark or wound or injury.

"Do what Handsome said," said Jeff to the three and indicating that they should move along the shore to retrieve a token from the clutch. No sooner had they moved than the lizard, running high on its legs, scurried to the turtle's side.

"Get on Handsome's shell," it ordered Jeff, who immediately obeyed. Two things now happened simultaneously. First, the gull alighted on Jeff's outstretched arm, and second, iguana wriggled to the front, just ahead of the stationary tortoise.

When the patrol was almost on top of them, the lizard raised up on its rear legs, extended its red tongue, and puffed out a scaly frill of a collar.

"Stop if you value your lives," said the bird who immediately turned toward Jeff and managed something that looked like a wink from his lidless right eye. "You are in the presence of the four Handsomes. Drop your weapons and cease your charge."

To Jeff's surprise they did.

"What do you see before you?" said the gull, "I'll tell you: *one who is not too ugly to eat you*, *one whose relentless pursuit is not too slow to wear you down for capture*, and *one who is not too fast for this human to catch!*"

The last remark made Jeff feel like it was some sort of introduction and he was to speak next.

"Why have you approached so recklessly and unannounced?" he said feigning the arrogance that they had heard often. "Do you wish to join us?"

"We are the guard of the White Samurai of the Rising Moon!" came a chorus.

"And when have you *ever* seen the moon rise in this sunlit place?" said Jeff. It was a simple enough observation, but one that completely perplexed the trio. They immediately sank to the ground and sat cross-legged on the beach.

"I ask you again: *Do you wish to join us?*"

"What will you do to us?" asked the captain who now considerably grassier than when Jeff last saw him. He had obviously claimed much of the grass the first group had left behind in the dungeon.

"We won't do anything *to you*! But we will do something *for you*! We offer transportation, safe passage to a better place than this."

"How do we know it's not a trap? How do we know you're not sending us to a worse place, a place where we will be slaves?"

"Is a worse place possible?" asked iguana who had relaxed after his ferocious posturing.

"Aren't you slaves here?" asked tortoise.

"But we have made names for ourselves!" said the captain.

"And in the place where the boat will take you, your true name will be spoken and remembered," said Jeff. How he knew this or felt this, he did not know, but the words came out of him with certainty. "You go to a place where life *is*, and not this one where it only *appears to be.*"

There was no further discussion, only surrender, and it took the form of three people tearing away their grassy exteriors to reveal, as Jeff thought, three very pleasant sorts of characters. With instruction from the gull, they followed iguana to the clutch and then to the rocky stairway that led to the grotto and the safely moored boat.

Once all had boarded, the bird took to the air and announced that there were no other sails on the horizon. The work of the four Handsomes was done, at least for a time. When the Handsome alighted close to Jeff, it spoke in a lower voice.

"I see many things from the air," it said. "At the edge of the trees is a haystack with ears. It may be that *your* work is not done."

"But your time must be," said the iguana returning from escort duty. "The shimmering is flickering."

"Can you see it?" asked Jeff anxiously.

"Yes," said tortoise. "In our time, we each had our own. Our portals have closed during our service here. Perhaps the next boat will be ours."

"But my portal is still active," said Jeff.

"For now," agreed turtle, "but I doubt you'll need it much longer."

Jeff would have liked to argue the point, but he was back in a hospital room. He did not remember going through the shimmering, but perhaps he did.

## Chapter 13

## Gloomy Day

"You've been far away!" Samantha was very gently stroking Jeff's cheek.

"You're beautiful," he said trying to focus his eyes on her but then being drawn to a window looking out on an overcast day and falling rain. "The weather is nice."

"You at least have your sense of humor back. It's an awful day."

"Rain is sweet," he heard himself say. "It gives life." He should have been surprised by how fluent his speech patterns were, but he had been so long in the other place that he expected his words to make sense.

"I feel so weak," he said struggling to keep his eyes open. With great effort he reached up to wipe a tear from Sam's cheek.

He recoiled at the sight of his own arm, black and blue with scaly deep bruises and bleeding sores. "What happened?"

Samantha would have liked to find her cheery voice, but it would not come. "Your clot medicine is out of whack. You've been bleeding inside. They've given you some medicine to counteract it, but you have to hold on."

Her pleading brought a smile to his face. "I love you," he said. "Sometimes we hold onto the wrong things and the wrong fears. Sometimes you can't even hold onto a name. Tell Brent and Megan that I love them, too."

He was gone.

## Chapter 14

# Final Sail

"We thought you'd return soon," said the iguana. Jeff was looking out toward the sea. It was a perfectly sunny day, and there was a sail on the horizon.

"Another boat is coming," said Jeff.

"Yes, it's the boat for the four Handsomes," said the reptile, "at least that's what we figured when four tokens appeared on the beach."

Jeff looked to his right saw only smooth stones and sand, no shimmering. In that moment he felt great loss, but not regret. He looked across the water. Going back was not his to choose, and staying here was not his to desire.

"The shimmering has stopped," said iguana. "I am sorry for that, but will be glad for your good company. Come with me and claim your token."

The two seemed an odd pair as they walked along, an upright man with a vertical axis and a crawling reptile providing the horizontal.

"Why did this happen?" he asked.

"I figured that you humans were better with the *whys* than we reptiles," said the animal. "I always tried to be satisfied with the things that *are*."

Jeff laughed. "And that's why you are handsome, the best looking *you* that ever existed."

"That fits us all, doesn't it?" said the iguana who scooped up what appeared to be a white beach stone from the two left. "The other two have been here already."

Jeff bent down and took the last of the tokens in his hand. It was pleasant to the touch and felt as though there was life in it. "I'll catch up with you at the boat," he said. "I want to take one more look around."

"You can't help him," said the lizard.

"I know, but he's still there."

"Yes, he's been watching since you left. He's shed his skin, you know?"

Jeff realized what iguana meant by the last comment. He was going to meet a man back at the tree line and not a haystack, certainly not the White Samurai of the Rising Moon.

He looked along the edge of the sterile façade, and there he stood. He was perhaps the smallest of the seven, made larger by his grass stuffing which he had now set aside.

"You look better that way," said Jeff when the two met.

"I didn't use to think so," said the man. "I guess it made me feel bigger." He paused thoughtfully before continuing. "I heard what the others told you about me wanting a horse. As I listened, I realized that they did not understand what I really wanted. I know that you'll leave soon, and I will be more at peace if I knew that someone understood."

"They said you wanted a horse to ride."

"That's just it," he said, "I wanted a horse for these." He reached into a pocket and brought out a handful of seeds that looked like kernels of corn or some other grain. "I needed a horse to plow," he added.

Jeff's expression softened and the man continued.

"When I heard everyone talking, I remembered that I was a farmer in some other place. I remembered coming here and finding nothing alive, but I had something that could be alive in my pocket." He looked at the seeds.

"What do you see there in your hand?" asked Jeff.

"Everything! I see stalks high over my head. I remember that I used to prop them up after a windstorm or heavy rain knocked them down. I see them becoming strong again, and that after the harvest we would cut paths through the field and make a maze so the children could play and the young lovers could steal kisses.

"I remembered it all, and wanted you to know."

To this day, Jeff could not tell you why he did it, but he did. He reached into his own pocket and pulled out the white token. "I'll trade you," he said.

"You can't," said the man.

"Can't I? Life for life seems fair to me. One day, perhaps I will plant them."

The man gingerly lifted the white stone that seemed to be pulsing, and carefully, without dropping a single grain, poured the seeds into Jeff's other hand.

"Hurry!" called the three Handsomes from the deck of the boat in the grotto. If they thought Jeff's exchange with the man a mistake, it did not show as they welcomed him aboard. Jeff saw the great sail being raised to a height above the sides of the grotto. Without a hint of wind, it filled and the boat began to take to the sea. The sail bore a single emblem, a white sand dollar outlined on a purer white sail.

He was standing very nearly in the spot where he was when he first came to the island. A golden holograph reminded him that he had taken something away, something that he was meant to return.

"Is this going to be your last regret?" Samantha was next to him holding a sand dollar. She was more beautiful than he remembered.

"If you are here, what regret can there be?" he asked taking the sand dollar from her and setting it down in the marked spot which quieted into peace.

"Time to go home," she said. As Jeff looked out to sea, her gaze followed his. *"Our home,"* she said, "at least for now. The children are anxious to see you. You did promise them a story."

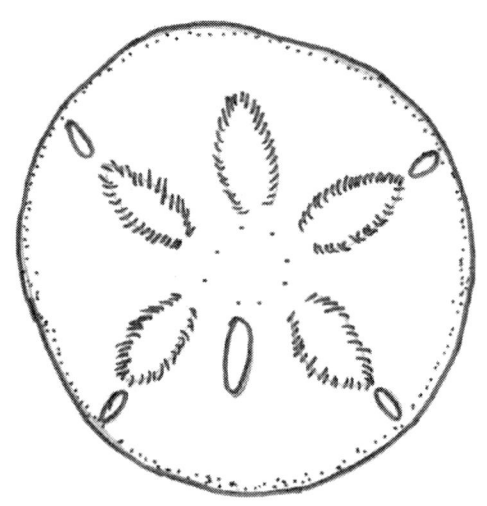

## Chapter 15

## Back in the World

I had promised a story for Megan and Brent, and I wasn't very far into the telling when they asked me to draw a picture. They did not want to see anything of the car or the twisted wreckage, but were curious about the Handsomes, the Grieves, and an island that never saw nightfall.

"We already have your drawings," I told them, but they were not satisfied.

"You draw something, too," they said. It took me awhile to be convinced.

At first I tried to think of a friend with the talent to render a reasonable image on a page, but nothing about the adventure seemed reasonable enough to explain. This proved true when I asked my niece to make a sketch. Her drawings were fine, but her imagination took the ink in directions which didn't look at all familiar.

I remembered the grotto where crude pictographs morphed into photographic quality. That's when I got the nerve to take up a felt-tipped marker and scratch an image on the page. Maybe some reader will stare long enough at the page that they will see more in these images than my talent could ever render. If you are that reader, don't be surprised to find that you are the Handsome in the picture.

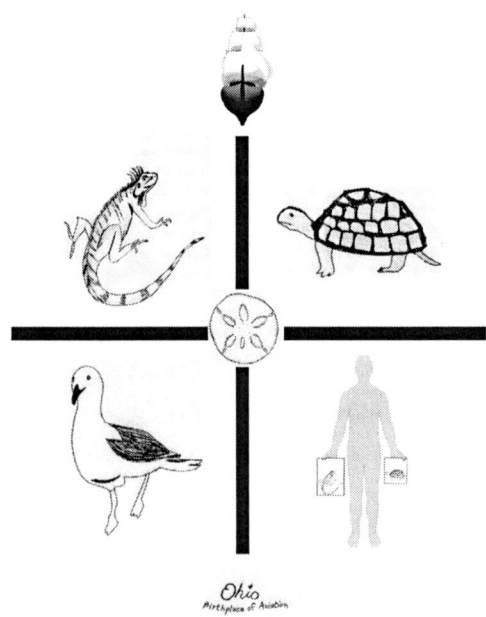

Rob Smith currently lives and writes on Ohio's north coast. He enjoys sailing, and when not working on his novels, he is refurbishing an 1850's house which was built by a ship's carpenter turned lighthouse keeper. In addition to his prose, he is also known for his poetry. In 2006 he won the Robert Frost Poetry Award from the Frost Foundation in Lawrence, MA. His undergraduate degree is from Westminster College in Pennsylvania and his master and doctoral degrees are from Princeton Theological Seminary.

To learn more about the author, visit his website at: SmithWrite.net

PHOTO CREDIT:
NANCY SMITH

CPSIA information can be obtained at www.ICGtesting.com
Printed in the USA
BVOW070107180113

310889BV00001B/1/P